The Spook Matinee

THE SPOOK MATINEE

and Other Scary Poems for Kids

Written and illustrated by GEORGE ULRICH

DELACORTE PRESS   NEW YORK

For Suzanne

Published by
Delacorte Press
Bantam Doubleday Dell Publishing Group, Inc.
666 Fifth Avenue
New York, New York 10103

Library of Congress Cataloging in Publication Data

Ulrich, George.
   The spook matinee: and other scary poems for kids / written and
illustrated by George Ulrich.
        p.   cm.
   Summary: A collection of short poems about such scary topics as
ghosts, spiders, aliens, vampires, and horror movies.
   ISBN 0-385-30552-4
   1. Horror—Juvenile poetry.   2. Children's poetry, American.
[1. Horror—Poetry.   2. Humorous poetry.]   I. Title.
PS3571.L72S66   1992
8911'.54—dc20   91-28270   CIP   AC

Typography by Lynn Braswell

Manufactured in the United States of America

October 1992

10 9 8 7 6 5 4 3 2 1

Contents

Getting There

Dracula the vampire
Sleeps in his coat and hat.
When he gets up to go to work
He turns into a bat.

Zombies lurch and stagger,
Goblins take the bus,
Wizards ride the subway
Just like the rest of us.

Witches fly on broomsticks.
Mummies take the train.
Frankenstein rides a bicycle
While looking for his brain.

There are many ways to travel.
I've tried out quite a few
And found it's better not to know
Who's sitting next to you.

Tigers Don't Scare Me

I'm not afraid
When a ghostly shade
Or vampire shrieks at me.
When gruesome ghouls
Chase me to school
It fills my heart with glee.

I keep my nerve
When a charging herd
Of tigers finds my path.
But I shake and frown
When Mrs. Brown
Quizzes us in math.

Take Me to Your Teacher

Alien spaceships came to Earth
Behind our school today.
We got to go home early
When they took Mrs. Brown away.

Going Uptown

One day in Riley's Petting Zoo
The elephant got loose.
He trampled on the pony cart
And trod upon the goose.

He ran around the duck pond
Pounced on the peacock's tail;
The keeper tried to shoo him back
But 'twas to no avail.

He raced through the gate and left the zoo.
(He left it in a fuss.)
And ambled down to Elm and Vine
To take an uptown bus.

The bus roared through the city,
The traffic beeped and honked.
The elephant got off to meet
His cousin in the Bronx.

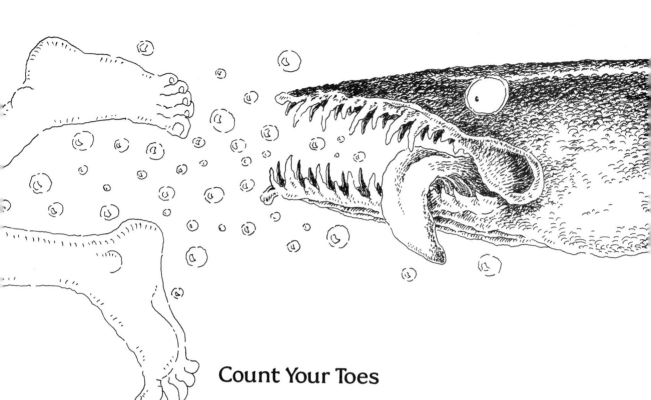

Count Your Toes

Of all the creatures in the sea
The one that I'd most like to be
Is the fearsome barracuda
Eating bathers in Bermuda.

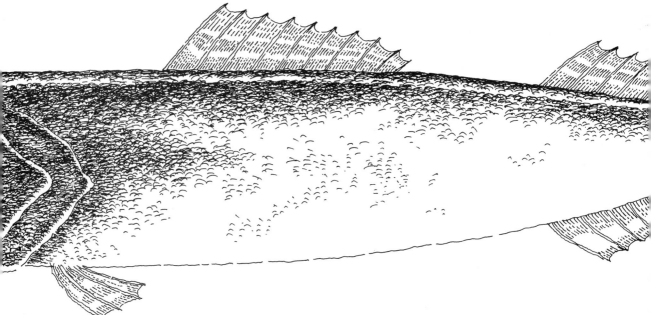

Splash!

Splashing in her wading pool
Suzie made a fuss.
For hiding in the water
Was a giant octopus.

Yo, Ho, Ho...

The phantom ship sails o'er the sea.
The crew's all ghosts and spooks.
They're singing nasty pirate songs
And reading comic books.

Zapped

The wizard waved his magic wand,
The sorcerer pulled his beard.
And when the smoke had finally gone
They both had disappeared.

In the Cellar

It's with some anguish I have found
A scary place where bears abound.
Nasty bears of green and yeller
Prowl the darkness of my cellar.

These bears will lurk and sneak and hide
From those poor souls who come inside
Their bone-strewn cavern, hidden lair,
The darkest place beneath the stair.

So when Mom says, "Be a good feller,
And get me something from the cellar,"
I close my eyes, descend the stairs,
Tiptoeing past those awful bears.

I see dark shadows on the wall
Hear shuffling feet and growly calls,
I grab the thing Mom sent me for,
Race up the stairs and slam the door!

Table Manners

A praying mantis sits to eat
Upon the dining table seat.
With fork and napkin near her plate,
She smacks her lips and eats her mate.

Bon Appétit

The spider with a leering mug
Pounces on a little bug.
With poison fang she bites her prey
Wrapping it in threads of gray.

This bound-up bundle, soft and still,
Hangs there in the web until,
Tiptoeing on her little feet,
Spider says, "It's time to eat."

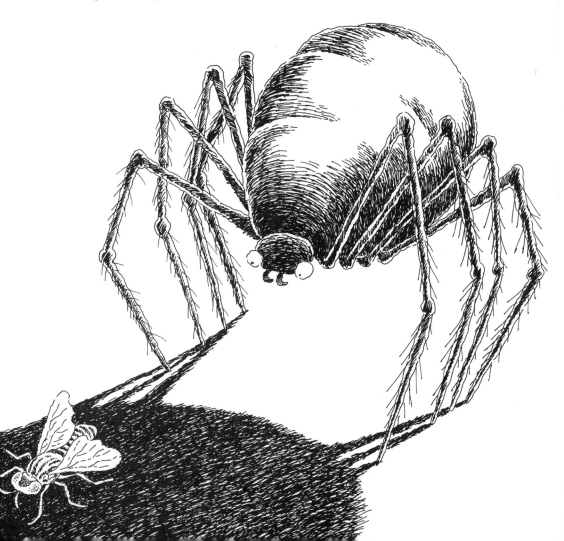

My Recipe

Some finely chopped-up monkey guts,
The eyeball of a fish,
Perhaps a tail of shredded snail
Will go into my dish.

I'll season it with bits of worms,
A pinch of sticky goo.
I'll pour it in a kettle, dear,
And cook it up for you.

My Favorite Snacks

I like to eat jam.
I like to eat jelly.
I like to eat worms
That tickle my belly.

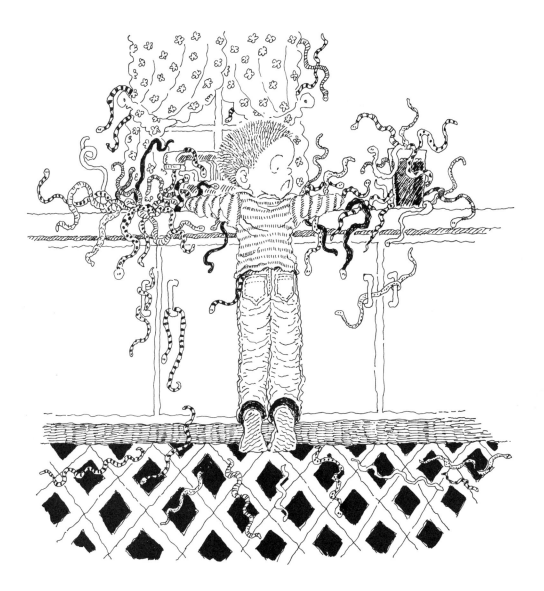

Crawlies

Creepy crawlies everywhere.
They're climbing in the sink.
They're wriggling in my ice cream,
And in my chocolate drink.

The Goblin

A goblin came to call today
And took my mother out to play.
Out she went against my wishes
Now *I* have to wash the dishes!

The Spook Matinee

I love horror movies,
They make my skin creep.
I sit down in front
On the edge of my seat.

While up on the screen
Ghouls rise from the mud,
Monsters wreak havoc,
And vampires suck blood.

Oh, I love being frightened,
It tops off my day
To be in this theater
At the Spook Matinee.

Home, Sweet Home

Trolls live under bridges.
Ghouls hang in trees.
Ogres crouch in tunnels,
And specters haunt the breeze.

It's spooky out there,
It's really a fright!
I'm going to stay home
And turn on the light.

If you think I'll go out
You've got rocks in your head.
I'll be in my bedroom
Hiding under the bed!

Tiptoe Through the Graveyard

I tiptoed through the graveyard,
I didn't make a sound.
I didn't want to wake the ghouls
Lying underground.

Just one small noise and they'd awake
And grab me by the hem.
They'd pull me down into the ground
And make me one of *them*. (Tra-la)

Say Cheese, Please

If a skull is empty bone
That once was someone's head,
Why is it when one grins at me
I feel a sense of dread?

Who's There?

Footsteps in the attic.
Moaning in the hall.
Peering 'round the corner
I see no one there at all.

Under the Bed

Hear it slither, hear it slink.
Imagine its tongue, long and pink,
Licking its slimy, snarling chops
And sharp white teeth, waiting to hop
On little Sally, George, or Ted
If they should tumble from their beds.

Take That!

I think I hear a monster coming,
Creeping near my bed!
I'll grab my feather pillow
And whack it on the head!

GEORGE ULRICH

has illustrated many books for young readers, including Stephen Mooser's The Creepy Creature Club series. He lives in Marblehead, Massachusetts, where he enjoys visiting old cemeteries and reading Stephen King novels.

The Spook Matinee and Other Scary Poems for Kids is the first book he has both written and illustrated.